VILLAINS ON THE LOOSE!

Tom McLaughlin
Paul Stewart

Pictures by
Bill Ledger

OXFORD
UNIVERSITY PRESS

OXFORD
UNIVERSITY PRESS

Great Clarendon Street, Oxford, OX2 6DP,
United Kingdom

Oxford University Press is a department of the University of Oxford.
It furthers the University's objective of excellence in research, scholarship,
and education by publishing worldwide. Oxford is a registered trade mark of
Oxford University Press in the UK and in certain other countries

British Library Cataloguing in Publication Data
Data available

9780192776105

1 3 5 7 9 10 8 6 4 2

Paper used in the production of this book is a natural, recyclable product
made from wood grown in sustainable forests. The manufacturing process conforms
to the environmental regulations of the country of origin.
Printed in China

Acknowledgements
Illustrations by Bill Ledger
Activities by Rachel Russ
Design by James W Hunter
Photo assets supplied by shutterstock.com, cgtrader.com, turbosquid.com.

CONTENTS

Helping your child to read

Before they start

- Talk about the back cover blurb. Ask your child why they think Wildcroft Woods might need to be saved.
- Look at the front cover. Ask your child to point to the two villains on the cover and describe them. What do they think they might be called?

During reading

- Let your child read at their own pace – don't worry if it's slow. They could read silently, or read to you out loud.
- Help them to work out words they don't know by saying each sound out loud and then blending them to say the word, e.g. *b-i-n-d-w-ee-d, bindweed*.
- Encourage your child to keep checking that they understand what they're reading. Remind them to reread to check the meaning if they're not sure.
- Give them lots of praise for good reading!

After reading

- Look at pages 37 and 71 for some fun activities.

CALLING ALL VILLAINS

Tom McLaughlin

Pictures by
Bill Ledger

In this story ...

Nisha
(**NIMBUS**)

Nisha has the power to control the weather!
She can make it sunny or stormy.
Once she used a hurricane to blow
away an army of robotic butterflies.

Cam
(**SWITCH**)

Cam has the power to turn into different
animals. She once stopped some baddies
from robbing a bank by turning into a giraffe.

1
IN A BIND

Nimbus struggled, but it was no use. **"I'M TRAPPED!"** she said to Switch.

Nimbus and Switch had been trying to stop the green-fingered villain Mr Brownleaf from robbing a bank, and now they were both caught in his super-strong bindweed.

Mr Brownleaf laughed. "Looks like you're *stuck* for ideas!"

Nimbus glared at Mr Brownleaf. "The only thing I hate more than bank robbers is bad jokes," she said. She managed to free one hand. Then she shot a layer of frost across the bindweed, which instantly froze. The bindweed shattered into hundreds of icy pieces, and Nimbus and Switch broke free.

Switch shape-shifted into a squawking
crow and dived towards Mr Brownleaf.

Mr Brownleaf took one look at Switch's
sharp beak and started to scream. "I hate
crows!" he cried, making a run for it.

Nimbus sprayed a sheet of ice along the ground hoping the villain would slip up.

Instead, Mr Brownleaf did a double twirl, followed by a jump. "**Ha, ha,**" he laughed. "You didn't know I won the Lexis City Ice Skating Championships three years in a row!"

With that, Mr Brownleaf skated off into the distance.

2
LEAFLET MYSTERY

"I can't believe he got away!"
Nimbus grumbled.

"Don't worry," said Switch, "we'll
get him next time. Let's get back to
Hero Academy."

"Wait. What's that?" Nimbus asked,
picking a leaflet up from the floor.

"Mr Brownleaf must
have dropped it," Switch
said. "What does it say?"

Nimbus read it
out loud.

CALLING ALL VILLAINS!

Want to take over the world?

Need some peace and quiet
to hatch a perfect plan? Want to meet
other like-minded baddies to discuss your
dastardly deeds?

If so, **Hotel Villain** is for you!

Come to the centre of Wildcroft Woods.

"Hotel Villain? That doesn't sound good," Nimbus said, with a frown.

"I think we should investigate," Switch replied.

"We can't go dressed like this," Nimbus pointed out. "The villains will recognise us. We need disguises."

Switch grinned. "**Good idea!**" she said.

3

WILDCROFT WOODS

An hour later, after raiding the Lost Property box at Hero Academy to get their disguises, Nimbus and Switch were trudging through the woods.

Switch stopped. "I've changed my mind," she said. "We look silly."

"I think we look **great!**" Nimbus replied, swishing her cape.

Nimbus and Switch crept deeper and deeper into the woods. The further they went, the gloomier it got. They ducked beneath spiky branches, trying not to get tangled in the trees.

"We must be nearly at the centre of the woods by now," Switch moaned.

Just then, they saw two large gates up ahead.

"That must be the hotel," Nimbus said.

"What now?" asked Switch.

"I suppose we could try knocking," Nimbus replied. She took a deep breath, then knocked on the gate three times.

The girls waited, but there was no answer.

Nimbus held out her hands. "Leave it to me," she said. I'll use a super-strong wind to blow the gates down."

"**NO!**" Switch cried. "You'll blow our cover as well."

KNOCK KNOCK KNOCK

Suddenly, they heard a voice coming from an intercom next to the gate. "Yes? Can I help you?"

"We're ... er ... villains. We've come to stay at the hotel," Switch said.

"Names?" the voice barked.

"I'm Cam," Switch said. Nimbus nudged her. Switch quickly added, "Cam-eleon! I'm Chameleon. I can disguise myself as anything."

"I'm Shade," Nimbus said. "I can blend into the shadows."

"Password?" demanded the voice.

Switch looked at Nimbus who shrugged.

Nimbus put on her best villain laugh. **"Mwah-ha-ha-ha!"**

There was no answer, but the gates silently swung open.

4
HOTEL VILLAIN

Nimbus and Switch stepped through the gateway and followed a winding path between some more trees.

They turned a corner, and Nimbus stopped and gasped. Rising up in the middle of the woods was the largest hotel she had ever seen.

The hotel was just as grand on the inside as it was on the outside. The reception area was filled with **DAZZLING** lights and **ENORMOUS** leather chairs.

Someone popped up from behind a desk to greet them. It was a small man wearing a green hat.

Nimbus gasped. It was Mr Brownleaf!

Mr Brownleaf glared at them. "Haven't I seen you two somewhere before?" he said.

"Er ..." said Switch.

"You probably recognise us from the Most Wanted Villains list," Nimbus jumped in.

"Hmm," Mr Brownleaf said with a grunt. "Are you staying here?"

"Not exactly. We'd like to speak to the owner," Switch said.

"He's very busy," Mr Brownleaf snapped.

Nimbus thought quickly. "We have a dastardly plan to get rid of Hero Academy!" she said.

Mr Brownleaf raised an eyebrow. "He'll want to hear *that*. Follow me."

Switch stared in wonder as Mr Brownleaf led them through the hotel. Everywhere she looked, she saw villains huddled in corners, plotting.

They went outside where there was
a large swimming pool. Someone was
floating in the middle on a rubber ring,
sipping a glass of iced orange squash.

Just then, a robotic bunny hopped
towards the side of the pool, holding a
plate of biscuits.

"A bunny-wunny," Switch muttered.
"That can mean only one person."

It was Ray Ranter, arch-enemy of Hero Academy.

"Welcome to Hotel Villain!" Ranter boomed from the pool. "You can stay here as long as you like."

"What's the catch?" Nimbus asked.

"You have to help me destroy Hero Academy once and for all."

"Great! That's exactly why we're here," Switch replied.

5

UNDER COVER

Ranter got out of the pool and quickly ducked into the changing room to put on his suit. Then he led Switch and Nimbus to a training room.

"What's that harmless little old lady doing here?" Switch whispered to Nimbus.

"Don't be fooled," Nimbus replied. "That's Silver Shadow. She's super-sneaky." Nimbus pointed to a man holding a feather duster. "And there's Mr Gleam. He's more dastardly than he looks, too."

"Attention, villains!" Ranter announced. "Today we will be learning to work as a team. It's the only way to defeat those troublesome heroes."

"But I like to work **alone!**" Silver Shadow cried out. "You lot would just slow me down," she said, glaring at the other villains around the room.

"**RUBBISH!** I could wipe the floor with you," said Mr Gleam, waving a duster at her.

"**As if!** I could knit you into knots!" said Silver Shadow.

"I'm not working with either of you," declared another baddie.

Soon, all the villains were yelling at each other.

"Why don't you lot just stop arguing?" Switch cried out.

Mr Gleam stared at her in shock. "But we're villains. Arguing is what we do."

Silver Shadow peered at Nimbus and Switch. "What did you say your names were?"

Nimbus tried to smile. "I'm Shade and this is Chameleon."

Mr Brownleaf came into the room, frowning. "I just checked, and there's no one called Chameleon or Shade on the Most Wanted Villains list."

Mr Gleam glared at them. "You're not villains. You're here to spy on us!"

Ranter gasped. "**Get them!**"

6
SUPER TWISTER!

The crowd of angry villains charged towards Nimbus and Switch.

As quick as a lightning flash, Nimbus summoned up a tornado.

"**ARGH!**" Mr Gleam screamed, as he was sucked into it.

"**NOOO!**" Silver Shadow cried, as she lost her grip on a table and went flying into the air.

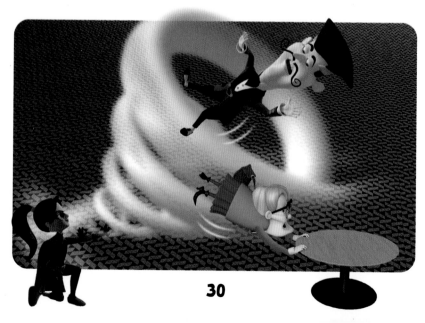

The tornado twirled and whirled around
the room. The villains were trapped inside it.

"SWITCH!" Nimbus bellowed. "OPEN
THE DOOR!"

Switch turned towards the door, but it
was already open.

Ranter was making his escape!

"I'll get Ranter," Switch yelled. "You send this lot to Lexis City."

Nimbus concentrated hard, then sent the tornado and the villains out of the door, through the woods and straight towards Lexis City Police Station.

Switch raced outside after Ranter.

"You'll never catch me!" Ranter laughed, looking over his shoulder.

Switch stopped. "Oh dear," she shouted back. "You should always watch where you're going!"

"**What?**" Ranter turned around to see the pool right in front of him. He tried to stop, and wobbled for a moment before landing in the water with a giant **SPLASH!**

Switch took a running jump, shape-shifted in mid-air and dived into the water.

"Argh! A shark! Help!" Ranter cried out. Nimbus watched from the side of the pool. "No one's going to help you," she replied. "The rest of the villains are gone, and the police are on their way."

Two weeks later ...

Ray Ranter appeared in the lounge of
the newly decorated Wildcroft Woods
Retirement Village. The room was full of
old people who were looking up at him
eagerly. As well as giving up his hotel,
Ranter had to help look after and entertain
the residents three times a week.

"Come on, Mr Ranter," said one man with a toothless grin. "You promised us a sing-song."

"Again?" Ranter moaned. "Oh all right." Ranter put down his tray, muttering to himself. "I should never have agreed to this."

Ranter sat down. "All **together now** ..." he groaned, starting to shake his tambourine.

AFTER READING ACTIVITIES

QUICK QUIZ

See how fast you can answer these questions!
Look back at the story if you can't remember.

1) Who are Nimbus and Switch trying to catch at the beginning of the story?

2) What is the password to open the hotel gates?

3) What does Nimbus summon to capture the villains?

THINK ABOUT IT!

How do you think Nimbus and Switch feel when the villains discover that they are there to spy?

SPOT THE DIFFERENCE

Spot the four differences between the pictures of the tornado.

37

RACE FOR THE METEORITE

Paul Stewart

Pictures by
Bill Ledger

In this story ...

Pip
(**BOOST**)

Pip is super strong! She can lift up really heavy weights, like boulders. She once lifted a skyscraper!

Jin
(**SWOOP**)

Nisha
(**NIMBUS**)

Mrs Molten
(**TEACHER**)

THE SOPHOS COMET

The **Sophos Comet** is a vast ball of ice and space rock that whizzes around the solar system. Unlike other comets, it is thought to be made from powerful, super-charged rocks.

Every five years, the Sophos Comet flies past Earth causing a **meteor shower** (where space rocks called meteors make streaks of light in the night sky). Anyone born during this meteor shower has the gift of superpowers.

Occasionally, during a meteor shower, a chunk of the meteor lands on Earth and becomes a meteorite. **Sophos Meteorites** are special because the super-charged rock can boost superheroes' powers. Some people even believe they can *give* you superpowers.

1
THE METEOR SHOWER

Ray Ranter was standing on a balcony of Ranter Tower, staring up at the night sky.

"If only I had superpowers like those pesky heroes," Ranter said. "I could take over Lexis City once and for all."

Just then, a ball of yellow light hurtled across the sky.

Ranter gasped. "**A METEOR!** Maybe it's from the Sophos Comet. It could give me the superpowers I need!"

Meanwhile, at Hero Academy, the superheroes saw the meteor streak down from the sky, too ...

In another part of Lexis City, Boulderman was on the roof of Rock House. He also watched the meteor pass overhead.

"I'm going to find that meteorite," he growled. "And when it has boosted my powers, I'll **DESTROY** Hero Academy once and for all!"

Many years ago, Boulderman had been a pupil at Hero Academy. Unfortunately, Boulderboy – as he was called back then – was often in trouble ...

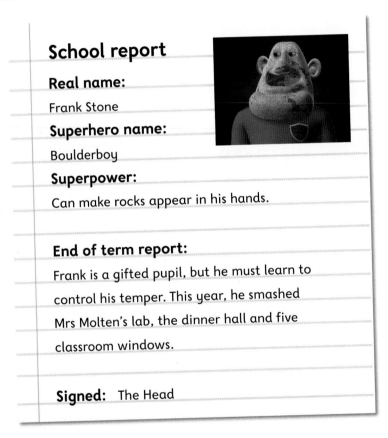

School report

Real name:

Frank Stone

Superhero name:

Boulderboy

Superpower:

Can make rocks appear in his hands.

End of term report:

Frank is a gifted pupil, but he must learn to control his temper. This year, he smashed Mrs Molten's lab, the dinner hall and five classroom windows.

Signed: The Head

Boulderboy felt that the Head was being unfair and he left Hero Academy, never to return.

2

A WALK IN THE WOODS

"Quick! Everyone off," Mrs Molten said, as she parked the school bus at the edge of Wildcroft Woods.

Nisha jumped off the bus. She spun into her superhero costume and became Nimbus. Beside her, Jin and Pip were soon dressed as Swoop and Boost.

Mrs Molten rummaged in the storage locker of the bus for the gadgets she'd brought to help find the meteorite. "Here, take this heat locator," she said to Swoop.

"Boost, I have a metal detector for you. Last but not least ... " She handed Nimbus an extra-terrestrial tracker to detect space material.

Just before they set off, Nimbus noticed two cars in the car park. "Do you think they belong to villains?" she asked.

"If they do, they've already got a head start," Boost replied.

"We haven't a moment to lose," Mrs Molten said, urgently. "That meteorite must **NOT** fall into the wrong hands."

As they went into the woods, the sound of birdsong filled the air. Then, suddenly, they heard something else.

BLEEP. BLEEP. BLEEP ...

"My metal detector," said Boost excitedly.

Moments later, Swoop's heat locator started to **buzz**. Then Nimbus's extra-terrestrial tracker let out a shrill **whistle**. Soon, the woods echoed with the **bleeping, buzzing, whistling** din.

"The meteorite must be somewhere over there!" said Nimbus. As she pointed, a **ZIGZAG** bolt of lightning shot out from her fingertips. Nimbus cried out with surprise. "My whole body's tingling," she said.

"So is mine," replied Swoop.

"*And* mine," said Boost. She leant against a tree to rest for a moment ... and pushed it over. "**WOW!**" she exclaimed. "I'm stronger than ever."

"It's the Sophos Meteorite," said Mrs Molten. "As we get closer, it's super-charging your powers." She frowned. "It must be nearby. I wonder why we can't see it?"

"I'll take a look," said Swoop. He jumped off the ground, then soared up into the air, so fast that the others lost sight of him in seconds. Moments later, he was back beside them.

"I didn't see the meteorite," he said
breathlessly, "but that was **A-MA-ZING!**
I flew so fast and so high, I almost went
into orbit!"

"You must all be careful, and try to
control your super-charged powers,"
Mrs Molten warned them. "Otherwise,
who knows what might happen?"

Just then, Nimbus sneezed.
Hailstones the size of tennis balls came
HAMMERING down from the sky.

"Sorry," she muttered, as she stopped
the hail shower.

3
DEEPER INTO THE WOODS

"Let's move on," Mrs Molten said. "Quickly now, and keep a sharp lookout. If there are any villains about, they might have set traps."

Mrs Molten strode ahead, with Nimbus close behind her. Swoop followed next, and Boost was at the back. They all walked as fast as they could through the dense undergrowth.

"We *must* be getting near the meteorite by now," Boost shouted above the bleep-bleep of her metal detector. "I ... **AAARGH!**"

She had trodden on a net that was hidden beneath some leaves. The net had shot up into the air with Boost inside. Now she was **trapped!**

Boost looked miserable. Swoop flew up and hovered next to her.

"I'll soon get you out of there," he said. Then he called down to Mrs Molten and Nimbus. "You go on. We'll catch you up."

Mrs Molten frowned. "I'm not sure about leaving you."

"This proves there are villains around. You have to find that meteorite before they do!" Boost cried. "Every second counts."

"Boost is right," Nimbus said.

Mrs Molten sighed. "All right. Be careful!"

She and Nimbus carried on through the woods, but it wasn't long before they ran into problems of their own.

"That's strange," Mrs Molten said. "It seems to be getting foggy."

"It's not me this time," Nimbus replied.

"Could you make it go away?" Mrs Molten asked.

"I'll try," said Nimbus. She summoned a breeze, but the fog wouldn't clear.

They **stumbled**. They **tripped**. They cried out.

"I can't see a thing!" Nimbus exclaimed. "Mrs Molten, where *are* you?"

"Over here!" came the reply, but Mrs Molten's voice was faint.

They were getting separated.

"Mrs Molten?" called Nimbus. "**Mrs Molten!**"

There was no reply. Nimbus was on her own.

Telling herself to be brave, Nimbus kept going. Then she heard a low **hum** up ahead.

Nimbus followed the noise and –
THUNK! – bumped into a large, metal box.

Attached to the box was a long funnel, with fog pouring out of it. Nimbus spotted a nameplate on the side of the box: Property of Ray Ranter.

"I might have known," Nimbus muttered. "I can guess why Ranter is using a fog machine – he's after the meteorite." She turned off the machine, and the air slowly cleared. "Now I need to find that villain, and fast!"

4
THE CLEARING

Nimbus took a deep breath. It was up to her to find the meteorite.

Just then, Nimbus spotted some footprints. She followed them until she could see a clearing up ahead. Then she heard the sound of raised voices. She hid behind a tree and peered round it.

There was the meteorite! It was half-buried in the earth. The ground around it was **steaming**.

There were also two people in the clearing. One of them was Ray Ranter, but Nimbus didn't recognize the other one. Tall and powerfully built, he looked as though he was made of rock. He and Ranter were arguing.

"I see you managed to avoid my traps," Ranter snarled. "No matter. I'll deal with you now, Boulderman."

"You'll never defeat me!" Boulderman bellowed. "You don't even have any superpowers."

"Soon I will. This meteorite will give them to me," Ranter told him.

Boulderman roared with laughter. "No it won't! You only get powers if you're born during a Sophos Comet meteor shower."

"That's what you think!" Ranter fumed.

"The meteorite is mine!" Boulderman shouted. "I'm going to become bigger and badder than ever. Then I'll **DESTROY** Hero Academy!"

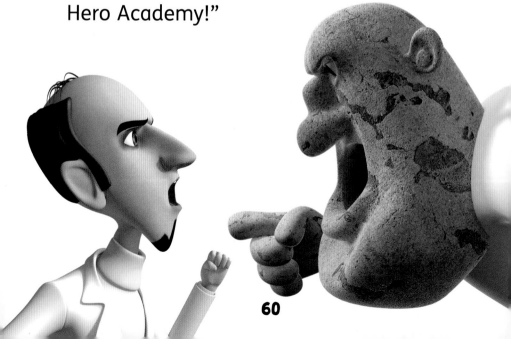

"If anyone's going to destroy Hero Academy," Ranter yelled back, "it'll be me."

Nimbus shuddered. She had to stop them at all costs.

"Stay away from that meteorite," Ranter warned.

"Or what?" Boulderman demanded.

"**Or this!**" cried Ranter.

Nimbus gasped. Suddenly, a bunch of bunny-wunnies emerged from the trees. They started to pelt Boulderman with carrots.

Boulderman stumbled back. He clapped his huge hands together and an **E-NOR-MOUS** rock appeared.

Boulderman was about to throw it at Ranter when the bunny-wunnies leaped up and tickled him. Boulderman shrieked with laughter and dropped the rock. It fell to the ground, sending a shower of dirt all over Ranter.

"My beautiful white suit!" Ranter cried out. He glared at Boulderman. "Nobody messes up my suit. You'll regret that!"

As the battle continued, Nimbus turned her attention to the meteorite. It still looked too hot to handle and much too heavy to move.

Nimbus raised her hands and concentrated hard. Seconds later, it began to pour with rain. It wasn't just any old rain, though. With her super-charged powers, Nimbus created rain that was so **hard** and so **HEAVY**, it poured down like a waterfall.

Steam rose from the meteorite as it cooled. The clearing where Ranter and Boulderman were still fighting started to turn into mud.

As the ground became a muddy swamp, the two villains sank up to their ankles. They didn't seem to notice, though. They were too focused on stopping each other getting to the meteorite.

Still hidden behind the tree, Nimbus waited. When Ranter and Boulderman were knee-deep in the thick mud, she put the second part of her plan into action. Nimbus stopped the rain and turned the air ice-cold.

"I can't move!" Boulderman yelled, as the mud froze solid.

"Neither can I!" Ranter whined.

"Now for the meteorite," Nimbus said to herself. She closed her eyes and concentrated, until she could hear a rush of wind. Then she opened her eyes and smiled. She had created a **whirlwind!** Nimbus pointed it at the meteorite. The whirlwind moved towards it and, with a loud **POP**, plucked the meteorite from the earth.

The meteorite hovered in the centre of the whirlwind, and Nimbus steered it out of the clearing and into the trees.

Stuck in the frozen mud, Ray Ranter and Boulderman could only stare as the meteorite swirled away.

As Nimbus and the whirlwind headed into the woods, she heard the two villains arguing.

"This is your fault!" Boulderman roared.

"No, it's your fault!" Ranter snarled back.

"Your fault!"

"Your fault!"

Nimbus left them to it. Keeping the spinning whirlwind under control, she made her way back through the trees. When she reached the car park, she saw the others standing next to the school bus.

"I've been so worried!" Mrs Molten exclaimed. "We tried to find you, but it was hopeless in all that fog."

Nimbus lowered her hands. The whirlwind stopped spinning and the meteorite dropped lightly to the ground.

"You got it!" Swoop said.

"Nice work, Nimbus!" Boost said, smiling.

5
BACK AT HERO ACADEMY

The Head congratulated Nimbus on finding the meteorite. "All the best meteorites have a special name," he said. "Nimbus, as you found it, you shall have the honour of naming it."

"How about the Sophos Super-charger?" Nimbus suggested.

The Head agreed that it was the perfect name. "It's so powerful that I'm going to lock it away safely," he said. "It can't cause any harm in my reinforced vault."

At least, that's what everybody hoped ...

AFTER READING ACTIVITIES

QUICK QUIZ

See how fast you can answer these questions!
Look back at the story if you can't remember.

1) Who becomes trapped in the net?

2) What do the bunny-wunnies throw at Boulderman?

3) What does Nimbus name the meteorite?

THINK ABOUT IT!

Why do the heroes have to be careful to control their super-charged powers?

IMAGINE IT

If Nimbus hadn't been there to stop Ray Ranter or Boulderman, what do you think would have happened? Why?

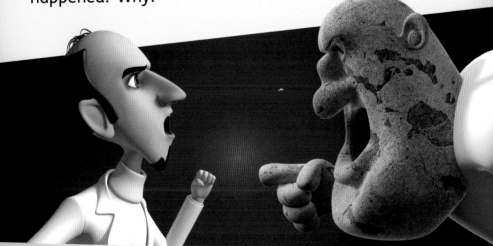

Answers: 1) Boost;
2) the Sophos Super-charger; 3) carrots.